GRuBtown
Book Five

Trick Eggs aNd
RubbeR ChickeNs

or

Making a Splash

A bit about the author

Philip Ardagh, whose very first GRuBtoWN taLe won him the Roald Dahl Funny Prize, is author of numerous books including the award-winning Eddie Dickens adventures, which have been translated into over 30 languages. He wrote BBC Radio's first truly interactive radio drama, collaborated with Sir Paul McCartney on his first children's book and is a 'regularly irregular' reviewer of children's books for the *Guardian*. Married with a son, he divides his time between Tunbridge Wells and Grubtown, where he cultivates his impressive beard.

GRuBtoWN taLes
Book Five

TricK Eggs aNd
RubbeR ChickeNs

or
Making a Splash

by *Philip Ardagh*

Illustrated by *Jim Paillot*

ff

faber and faber

For John Boyne.
Yes, THE *John Boyne*

First published in 2010
by Faber and Faber Limited
Bloomsbury House
74-77 Great Russell Street
London
WC1B 3DA

Typeset by Faber and Faber Limited
Printed in England by CPI Bookmarque, Croydon

A CIP record for this book
is available from the British Library

ISBN 978–0–571–24793–6

2 4 6 8 10 9 7 5 3 1

A bit about Grubtown

You won't find Grubtown on any maps. The last time any mapmakers were sent anywhere near the place they were found a week later wearing nothing but pages from a telephone directory, and calling for their mothers. It's certainly a town and certainly grubby – except for the squeaky clean parts – but everything else we know about the place comes from Beardy Ardagh, town resident and author of these tales.

GRuBtoWN taLes were made possible through the participation of the following people, animals and organisations:

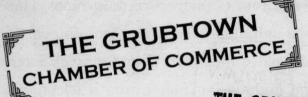

THE GRUBTOWN
CHAMBER OF COMMERCE

THE GRUBTOWN
CHAMBER OF
HORRORS

THE OFFICE
of the Mayor
of Grubtown

OFFAL'S
SUNBEDS

THE SHED
of the Mayor
of Grubtown

The Mayor
of Grubtown
Himself

THE GRUBTOWN
RIFLE
CLUB

THE GRUBTOWN
TRIFLE
(& JELLIES)
CLUB

THE GRUBTOWN
POLICE
DEPARTMENT

KILL ALL DUCKS

Wretching's Dairy

JIP
THE PELICAN
★ ★ ★
GRUBTOWN'S
OFFICIAL
MASCOT

GRUBTOWN
COASTGUARD
& DECKCHAIR
DEPARTMENT

THE RUSTY
DOLPHIN CAFE

CONTENTS

A cheery 'hello!'

I've been accused of being a bit of a grump-bag lately, so I thought I'd make this a hippy-happy-hoppy-bunnies kind of message.

'Greetings, kiddywinks! Here's the fifth lovely book about the lovely people of lovely Grubtown. Aren't you lucky?'

Oh, whooppeeeeeeeeeeeeeeeeeee!

Now get on with it.

Beardy Ardagh

Grubtown

1

The inhabitants
of Grubtown

At the back of the book (starting on page 117), you'll find a list of people living in Grubtown. If you want a longer list, then you'll have to get hold of a Grubtown telephone directory. You can't borrow mine because I'm using it. It's great for throwing at unwanted visitors before they even make it to my front door.

A word from
Beardy Ardagh

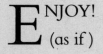NJOY!
(as if)

Beardy Ardagh

Grubtown

Yet another quick word (or twelve)

I don't care what you think. I'm NOT in a bad mood.

Chapter One
Rumble! Rumble!

The lorries delivering the sea creatures rumbled into Market Square (which is actually more round than a square). 'Rumble! Rumble!' they went.

Mango Claptrap leapt up and down excitedly, which was a particularly funny sight, what with him wearing those ridiculously short shorts of his. Next to him, Jilly Cheeter, his very best friend in Grubtown (and, therefore, the whole wide world), let out an excited squeal, rather

like the noise a pig might make if it won a free mud bath or a year's supply of potato peelings.

Neither Jill nor Mango had ever seen an octopus or a shark or a great big eely-thing (which might well have been a great big eel) in real life before, but here they were in enormous tanks strapped on to the backs of the lorries with special thick, black rubber straps.

Mango Claptrap waved at the octopus. Perhaps he was hoping the octopus would wave back, maybe even with all eight of its arms. (Or are they legs?)

Jilly and Mango weren't the only ones watching the arrival of the first inhabitants of the new **GRUBTOWN AQUARIUM AND CARWASH**. Many of the local ducks – including one called Orlando – had waddled into the square to catch the excitement, along with the usual mob of squawking seagulls.

Jip the town mascot and his partner Binkey – a pair of pelicans – came in to land on the railings surrounding one of the many statues of Big Man Gomez dotted around Grubtown. The pelicans studied the smaller fish in the tanks with a glassy stare that suggested that they were eyeing them up as a possible mid-morning snack. Not that either of them can have been that hungry because Mayor Flabby Gomez is always feeding them titbits.

The driver of the first lorry switched off his engine and the drivers of the three lorries snaking behind him did the same. The first driver jumped down from his cab, looked around the square, hitched up his baggy blue trousers and then ambled over to Jilly Cheeter and Mango Claptrap.

'I'm looking for Slackjaw Gumshoe,' he said. Slackjaw Gumshoe owns **SLACKJAW GUMSHOE'S**

PAINT & HARDWARE STORE over on Gibbon Street. (It used to be called Hillock Portal's Paint & Hardware Store, but that was back in the days when Hillock Portal owned it.) Slackjaw is also the person who had the bright idea of building **THE GRUBTOWN AQUARIUM AND CARWASH**.

No, that's not quite true. The aquarium had been his idea and when he presented it to a meeting of the town council, along with a big bag of money he thought the mayor might like as a present, it was Mayor Flabby Gomez who came up with the idea of the carwash. Slackjaw Gumshoe could keep all the money he made from the aquarium, but Flabby Gomez would get all the money for the carwashes.

('People always need clean cars but don't always need to see fish in tanks,' Mayor Gomez later explained to me. He's smart like that.)

'I saw Mr Gumshoe buying a cup of coffee over at the Rusty Dolphin Cafe,' said Jilly

Cheeter. She'd seen him going in there with Hacking-Cough Gomez, the mayor's brother, who'd won the contract to build the aquarium (and carwash).

'Well, he should be right here, right now,' said the driver angrily, as though it was somehow Jilly's fault that he wasn't. The driver's name was John Jones. It said so on a name tag sewn above the pocket of his shirt.

'Here comes Mr Gumshoe now.' Mango pointed. 'He's the one without the hacking cough.'

'Thanks,' muttered John Jones but he didn't sound like he meant it.

While the driver went over to talk to Gumshoe, Jilly Cheeter and Mango Claptrap went right up close to his truck and stared up at the tanks.

'That octopus is enormous!' said Jilly.

'Super-huge,' agreed Mango. 'He's brilliant!'

'Fantastic,' agreed Jilly. 'I wonder if we could

get jobs at the aquarium when it opens?'

'I expect you can,' said Mango Claptrap. 'You have experience working with animals.'

This is true. As some of you already know, Jilly Cheeter used to be Grubtown's official duck-gatherer. It was her job to round up all the ducks and put them in The Duck House.

'But everyone knows how good you are with animals too,' said Jilly, which is also true. One of the big companies in Grubtown is *Wretching's Dairy* and Mango Claptrap used to go and help with odd jobs there, such as taking the cows out for a walk, or taking stones from their hooves.

Hacking-Cough Gomez and Slackjaw Gumshoe wandered over to the truck with Jones the driver. Jones was frowning, Hacking-Cough appeared to be choking on a cappuccino – there was some frothy milk involved – and Slackjaw Gumshoe seemed deep in thought.

Gumshoe's eyes fell on the children, as if he'd

only just noticed that they were there. 'Ah!' he said, grinning a happy grin. 'You know the way to the new aquarium, don't you, Miss Cheeter?'

'Yes,' said Jilly Cheeter.

'We most certainly do,' said Mango Claptrap.

'Good,' said Slackjaw Gumshoe. 'Would you mind showing Mr Jones, here, the way?'

'Happy to oblige,' said Mango.

'Then jump in,' said John Jones as he climbed back into the cab of his lorry. Jilly and Mango scrambled up after him.

The building site that would soon be the aquarium was at the top of Clear-Day Hill. Clear-Day Hill was originally called You-Can-Get-Quite-A-Good-View-On-A-Clear-Day Hill because you could indeed get quite a good view of the sweeping bay around which much of Grubtown is built. (On a clear day.) It was Big Man Gomez who had renamed the hill. And no one dared argue with him.

The convoy of lorries came to a halt and Jones the driver gave another grunt of thanks to Jilly Cheeter and Mango Claptrap who'd shown him the way. They all jumped down on to the hard dry mud, worn flat by the tracks and tyres of the diggers, cranes, dumper trucks and lorries which had driven up and down, up and down the hill over the previous ten months.

The aquarium building was almost complete. Only a couple of months previously, it had been little more than an empty shell. Now the huge glass tanks were not only in place but also filled with water of exactly the right temperature. There were even inviting rocks and colourful friendly weeds in them.

'This place is amazing!' said Mango Claptrap.

At that moment a bright orange minibus drew up alongside the first lorry and a whole bunch of people piled out, each wearing bright orange clothes. It made them look a bit like traffic cones.

Jilly Cheeter and Mango Claptrap both recognised the one who was obviously in charge. It was none other than Farflung Heaps, leader of the Angry Mob, who has a house very near mine. (Mine is much nicer.)

He didn't look at all angry, though. In fact,

he looked smiley-happy.

'What are you doing here, Mr Heaps?' asked Jilly Cheeter.

'I'm in charge of getting all the animals safely into the right tanks,' said Farflung Heaps. 'When I'm not with the Angry Mob, running around with flaming torches and pitchforks, I'm a marine biologist.'

'Someone who knows all about sea animals?' asked Mango Claptrap.

'Precisely.' Farflung Heaps nodded.

'I never knew you were a marine biologist,

Mr Heaps,' said Jilly Cheeter with a well-you-learn-something-new-every-day expression on her face.

'That's why I live in Grubtown,' he explained. 'To be near the sea. The opening of the new Aquarium —'

'And Carwash,' Mango reminded him.

'— and Carwash,' said Mr Heaps, 'is the first time in ages I've had the chance to use my expert knowledge. But — if there's anything to get really angry about — I'm only a phone call away and still ready to lead the Angry Mob at very short notice.'

'Can we help?' asked Jilly Cheeter. 'With getting the fish and things into the tanks?'

'No, I'm afraid not, Jilly,' said Farflung Heaps. 'But you and Mango can watch.'

So they did. And had a great time.

Chapter Two
Clickerty-Clack

After many years and a great deal of wool, Flabby Gomez finally finished knitting his new house. Now he and his family were ready to move in. As Mayor of Grubtown, he used to live in the mayor's official residence, but this was ruined a long while back during the WORLD BEATERS' FESTIVAL. (This was the same festival that caused the hair of Mrs Awning's husband, Mr Awning, to turn white. This was the festival which made Chevvy Offal frightened of elbows to this day. You only have to say the word 'elbow' and he goes all funny-peculiar.)

The new house had been knitted from any wool that Mayor Gomez could lay his hands on: new wool bought from wool shops, old wool bought from second-hand shops; wool given by friends and relations; wool confiscated by police in the line of duty; wool washed up on the beach, dried and rolled in balls; bits of wool from old birds' nests tied into strands. Any way that Flabby Gomez could get wool without breaking the law, he did it. And if he found a way which WAS against the law, he simply changed the law so that it wasn't any more (if you see what I mean).

And now there was to be the grand opening ceremony as this knitted house was to become the mayor's official home. Gomez Heights, as Flabby had decided to name it, may not be the world's first knitted house – I've no idea – but it must be one of the most colourful. Because he used wool from here, there and everywhere, it's made up of just about every colour you can think of and some you have only ever caught a glimpse of on the very fringes of your imagination. (Perhaps in nightmares, or when your temperature was 120° and you were sucking your bedclothes and shouting very loudly about the bad rainbows coming to get you.)

To be honest for a change, looking at the house always makes me feel a little queasy. I think it's partly to do with the weird colour combination and partly due to the fact that not *one* of its walls is straight. What do

you expect? It's a ziggy-zaggy fluffy-edged KNITTED house.

Flabby Gomez is quite a laid-back chap. He doesn't really have a reason not to be relaxed about most things, I suppose. He owns Grubtown, and just about everyone – except his son, Tundra – does as he says, so he hasn't got much to get cross about. We were once trapped in a cake shop overnight together. He didn't panic. We just ate all the cakes and buns and played I'll Tickle Thomas, until we were found the next morning and let out. There was no shouting or banging or breaking of windows, just plenty of happy cake-eating.

When it came to discussing plans for the grand opening of Gomez Heights at a special meeting in his private chambers in Grubtown Town Hall, however, he seemed a bit tense. He really, really, *really* wanted the day to be a big success.

At the meeting with him were: Grabby

Hanson (the chief of police), Constable Gelatine (a police sergeant), Mustard Tripwire (a police officer and Gelatine's nephew), Rambo Sanskrit (Grubtown's official job-giver-outer), Pageant Conquest (chef and Grabby's sister) and me, Beardy Ardagh (international best-selling children's author).

Mayor Flabby Gomez sat in a saggy old armchair, with a big flabby grin on his big flabby face and Jip – the town mascot pelican – under one arm. Binkey, Jip's mate, sat outside on a ledge watching us all through the window.

'I want the grand opening of Gomez Heights to be spectacular,' said Flabby. 'I want Grubtowners to be talking about the day for years to come. I want both Grubtown papers* to bring out special editions, packed with photographs of the day, that people will carefully put away to show their children and their children's children.'

'What if they don't have any ch–?' began

*The Grubtown Daily Herald and
The Grubtown Weekly Gerald

Mustard Tripwire, until his Uncle Constable kicked him on the ankle, so he decided to say, 'OUCH!' instead.

Very loudly. And to rub his foot.

'And I don't want there to be any unfortunate mishaps,' the mayor went on, 'like we had when the film star Tawdry Hipbone came to town.'

'No, sir,' said Police Chief Grabby Hanson. He

remembered the day with a shudder, recalling the smell of fish which hung over the town for weeks afterwards.

Flabby Gomez turned to me. 'I want you to write a poem.' His eyes sparkled with the excitement of it all.

'I don't want to rain on your parade –' I began.

'Who told you about the parade?' demanded Chief Hanson. 'I thought that was a secret, Flabby?'

'I've told no one about the parade, Chief,' Flabby reassured him. He turned back to me. 'And what do you know about the weather?' he demanded. 'I thought it was going to be sunny on the 34th?' (In Grubtown, we use a slightly different calendar to the one you're probably used to.)

'"Rain on your parade" is a saying,' I explained. 'A figure of speech. What I meant was that I'm sorry to put a downer on things, but – er – I'm not actually a poet, Mr Mayor.'

'But you've written poems. I've read some,' said Pageant Conquest. 'You did that funny one about the goat in a boat.'

'It was a stoat in a moat,' I corrected her.

'So you DO write poems!' said Rambo Sanskrit. This was the first thing he'd said since he'd made himself comfortable on a huge pile of old knitting-patterns. He has very bushy eyebrows and very droopy eyelids so it's hard to tell when his eyes are open and when they're closed . . . and whether he's asleep or not.

'Yes,' I admitted, 'I do sometimes write the odd poem now and again, but they're not really *poemy* poems, if you know what I mean.'

Flabby Gomez struggled into a more upright position, his flabby body rippling in protest. 'But I *don't* know what you mean, Beardy,' he said.

'I mean that they're more ditties: shoe, glue, view-hulloo. . . That kind of thing.'

'Shoe? Glue? View-*what*?'

'View-hulloo,' said young Officer Mustard Tripwire, politely.

His uncle kicked him in the ankle again, probably for fun this time.

Flabby Gomez struggled to his feet, causing Jip to jump down on to his lap then straight off it, reluctantly waddling across the floor. 'I've no idea what you're talking about,' the mayor said. He looked around his private chamber.

'I expect you're more after a *On this special day and night, we rejoice in the opening of Gomez Heights*,' I said.

'Perfect,' said Mayor Flabby Gomez, who obviously has a poor ear for poetry. He turned to Rambo Sanskrit, who seemed to have produced a pen and spiral notepad out of nowhere. 'Make a note, Sanskrit. Beardy Ardagh, official poet on the day.'

Next he turned his attention to the no-longer-secret parade.

'We need costumes,' he announced.

The mayor loves parades and he loves costumes. A costumed parade *and* the grand opening of his home all in one day was his idea of heaven.

I was busy worrying about the poem I'd have to write and what I could rhyme with the word 'wool'.

Chapter Three
A bonk on the head

Those of you who've read a GRuBtoWN taLe or two before will be fully aware that Jilly Cheeter and Mango Claptrap are local celebrities. They may only be children, but they're children who've done great things. It's thanks to them that there's a fabulous diamond and a solid gold crown in Grubtown's museum, for example, and they've helped our town in so many other ways too.

If I liked children, I think Jilly and Mango would probably be the kind of children I'd like.

Helpful.

Polite.

Friendly.

And careful not to stand on my beard.

Flabby Gomez wanted Jilly and Mango to be a part of his parade at the grand opening of Gomez Heights, so he had told them to come to his office at 3 o'clock to discuss it (which would give him time to have a little snackette between lunch and the tea he planned to serve them at 3.15).

Unfortunately, Jilly Cheeter and Mango Claptrap were so busy watching Farflung Heaps and his crew carefully putting all the sea creatures in their new homes at **THE GRUBTOWN AQUARIUM AND CARWASH,** that they'd completely lost track of what time it was.

It was only when a clock fell on Mango's

head that they realised it was already ten past three.

Yup: clock.

Yup: fell on his head.

'Are you okay?' asked Jilly Cheeter. She was worried because this wasn't a *little* clock I'm talking about. This wasn't something you'd put on your bedside table. This clock was a BIG clock that was supposed to be easy for people to read the time on even when it was VERY high up on the wall and the people looking up at it

were

    way . . .

        way . . .

            way . . .

                down . . .

                    below.

Only now this clock wasn't high up anywhere, but lying on the aquarium floor having hit Mango and then bounced off him.

'I'm okay,' said Mango Claptrap, but he didn't sound sure of himself.

Farflung Heaps came running over. 'What happened?' he asked.

'That clock just fell off the wall and hit Mango,' said Jilly.

Farflung Heaps looked angry. And, as head of the Angry Mob, Heaps was particularly good at looking angry. 'That could have killed you,' he fumed. 'It could have landed in a tank and killed one of the animals.' When he said this last bit he looked even MORE angry.

He pulled a mobile phone out of his trouser pocket and punched in a number.

'Are you calling a doctor?' asked Jilly Cheeter.

Farflung Heaps shook his head.

'Are you calling the Angry Mob?' asked Mango Claptrap as he hauled himself to his feet. Luckily, the Claptrap family seem to have thick skulls.

'I'm calling Slackjaw Gumshoe to complain about the state of this aquarium!' said Heaps.

It was then that Jilly noticed that the time on the face of the smashed clock was ten past three.

'Yikes,' she said. Yes, she really did. Y-I-K-E-S. 'Is that the right time?'

'Is there ever a right time to have a clock land on your head?' slurred Mango Claptrap. He was seeing stars. Actually, he was seeing *sea* stars, a whole tank of them being carried from one of the lorries. Sea star is the correct name for starfish. Farflung Heaps had told them that earlier.

★ ★ ★

Jilly Cheeter and Mango Claptrap arrived at Grubtown Town Hall at a little after 4 o'clock and were in the mayor's office by 4.22. That was over an hour and twenty minutes later than he'd told them to be there.

The mayor would have been really annoyed if weren't for the fact that:

1. this had given him the opportunity to have the 3.15 tea all to himself
2. *and* the time to send out for extra biscuits
3. *and* to eat them too
4. and he was such a big fan of Jilly Cheeter and Mango Claptrap to whom he'd awarded plenty of medals in the past
5. *and* he was so very HAPPY at the thought of moving into his newly knitted home that nothing – not even

the late arrival of Jilly and Mango –
could spoil his mood.

'Welcome!' he said when the two children
were shown in. He looked closely at Mango
Claptrap. Then he looked again. 'Why are you
wearing a turban?' he asked.

'It's not a turban, it's a bandage, Mr Mayor,'
said Mango Claptrap, and went on to explain
about his accident.

'We must have Dr Fraud take a look at you
at once,' said Flabby Gomez. (Dr Fraud isn't a
real doctor, but he's so good at not being a real
doctor that nobody seems to mind.)

'He *has* seen him,' said Jilly Cheeter. 'Dr Fraud
was the one who bandaged Mango's head. He
did it on the bus on the way over.'

This was no word of a lie.

Now it was time to get down to business.
Mayor Gomez explained to Jilly Cheeter and
Mango Claptrap about the plans he had for

the day. He told them about everything from the skywriting, free ice cream and free carnival rides to the food sculptures. 'And, as two of our most honoured citizens, I want you both to lead a parade,' he said.

'Blimey!' said Mango Claptrap.

'Coo!' said Jilly Cheeter. 'What an honour.'

'Thank you, Mr Mayor,' said Mango. (When Flabby Gomez first elected himself mayor, he had people call him 'your worship' but, after a time, he began to suspect that some people – naming no names – were calling him 'your *war*ship' as a joke. So nowadays he has people call him 'Mayor Gomez', or 'Mr Mayor'.)

'You'll be wearing some very special costumes on the day,' said Flabby. 'I'm having them especially made for you by Gladrags and Stitch.'

'Blimey!' said Jilly Cheeter for a change.

'Coo!' said Mango Claptrap, because the 'blimey' had already been used up.

Gladrags & Stitch is a very famous costume company. For example, they made all the costumes for the live-action version of *102 Poodles*. (There'd have been no point in making costumes for the cartoon version, how would there? Drawings can't wear real costumes.)

'What are the costumes like, Mr Mayor?' asked Jilly, who'd been made to dress up as a duck by the mayor on more than one occasion, back in the days when she was our official duck-gatherer.

'It's a surprise,' said Flabby Gomez. 'You'll pick up your costumes on the morning of the parade.'

Chapter Four
Sun, Sea and Sand

When the morning of the grand opening of Gomez Heights finally came, Jilly Cheeter woke early. She was too excited to go back to sleep, so she decided to take Harvey, her dog, for a walk along the beach. Even Grubtown looks beautiful in the early-morning light, and the sun was already heating up the pavement.

It's a short distance to the beach from

the Cheeter house. It may not be the most fashionable part of the beach, where all the beautiful people go, but it still has the same golden sand, the same beautiful sea to the same horizon with the same sky above it.

Jilly unhooked Harvey's lead and he jumped up at her excitedly, doing a little doggy hind-leg dance. She picked up a large piece of driftwood, pulled off a few stubborn strands of seaweed, and threw it for Harvey to fetch. It was a bit bigger than the dog was used to so, as well as leaving paw prints in the sand, he left a line from where he'd dragged the stick.

Harvey seemed to like it best when Jilly threw the stick into the sea. He leapt up and down in the shallow water, the tide foam tickling his shaggy underbelly.

Jilly Cheeter was thinking about the grand opening of Gomez Heights. Well, she was thinking about the free ice cream and the carnival rides, and was wondering what costume **Gladrags & Stitch** had made for her. With any luck, it would be a fun day out.

She felt less happy when she saw a huddle of people walking towards her along the beach. It wasn't that she wanted to be alone. It had more to do with WHO it was that was walking towards her along the beach. It was Derek, Bunty, Shaun, Mantle, Fastbuck and Garrideb. In other words, the Fox family.

Very few people here in Grubtown like the Fox family. (Me included.) I suspect if the Foxes were better known, very few people in the WORLD would like the Fox family. They're not terribly – er – likeable. They hate ducks for starters, and no one in their right mind hates ducks.

What's to hate about them?

Think about it.

WHAT'S TO LIKE ABOUT DUCKS:

A. They make a brilliant quacking sound.

B. They really show their appreciation when you feed them bread. (If I gave my dad stale bread when he was in the bath, he wouldn't splash around all excitedly and come back for more.)

C. They walk with a comedy waddle.

D. They don't carry guns.(No arms.)

E. They're not afraid to look you in the eye.

F. Daffy and Donald are amazing cartoon
   characters and they're ducks.

NOTE: Okay, so if you're in a house
   full of ducks – such as The Duck
   House – they may smell a bit <u>ducky</u>
   sometimes, but a house full of
   humans can be as smelly as a rank
   swamp adder's armpit (if swamp
   adders had armpits).

There's *nothing* not to like about ducks, yet
the Fox family hates them. And they hate Jilly
Cheeter because she used to be Grubtown's
official duck-gatherer, whose job it is to look
after our feathered friends.

'It's the duck girl,' said Shaun Fox as they got
nearer.

'With her mangy dog,' said Derek and Bunty
Fox's only daughter, Garrideb.

Jilly Cheeter knew it was best to ignore

them, but she didn't like them being rude about Harvey.

She was just trying to think of something to say back to the Foxes – you know, a really good put-down to make them feel silly and small – when the sand just a few steps ahead of the Foxes began to move . . .

. . . and someone, or some*thing*, sat up, sand pouring off it.

Bunty Fox screamed.

Derek Fox said, 'What the –?'

Shaun Fox (the eldest son) just turned and ran.

Fastbuck took one step backwards in fright and fell over, which just left Mantle and Garrideb. Mantle didn't seem to notice what was happening because he was listening to music through his headphones and the glass in his dark glasses was so dark that he couldn't really see much anyway.

Gariddeb simply stared, open-mouthed and

dribbling, at the body that rose up out of the ground.

The 'thing in the sand' was none other than Hobo Browne, Grubtown's resident 'gentleman of the road'/'tramp'/'homeless person'.

'Hello, Miss Cheeter,' he said, grinning a rotten-toothed grin at Jilly. He was either totally unaware of the effect his sudden appearance had had on the Fox family, or he simply didn't care.

'Hi, Mr Browne,' said Jilly Cheeter. 'What were you doing buried in the sand?'

'Doing?' asked Hobo Browne, brushing the fine sand off his well-worn clothes. 'Oh, I see what you mean. I was sleeping. It's further up the beach than the tide ever reaches at this time of year, and this fine kind of sand makes excellent bedclothes.'

Jilly realised now that what she had mistaken for a small rock or a clump of seaweed had been Hobo Browne's head poking out of the top. He picked up a grey rolled-up vest which he'd used as a pillow. (And don't you go getting me into trouble by burying yourself in the sand at night. IT'S DANGEROUS.)

'There ought to be a law against you!' snarled Mr Fox. He looked from Hobo Browne to Jilly Cheeter and then back again. 'The pair of you ... frightening honest-to-goodness hard-working folk first thing in the day.'

He stomped off with such heavy footfalls that he made big, big dents in the sand. Bunty, meanwhile, was chasing after her boy Shaun.

Honest? thought Jilly. The Foxes hadn't been that long out of jail. *Goodness?* She wasn't sure there was an ounce of goodness in all of the Foxes put together. *Hard-working?* All any of them seemed to do was make models of dead or badly injured ducks for their stupid shop KILL ALL DUCKS, which never had any customers anyway.

At that moment, a bright blue truck with

SLACKJAW GUMSHOE'S PAINT & HARDWARE STORE

emblazoned on the side pulled up in There's-A-Mine-In-It Car Park at the top of the beach. A mine is a floating bomb which looks a bit like a giant conker still in its spiky case. There *is* actually a mine in There's-A-Mine-In-It Car Park, but the explosives were taken out over fifty years ago and it's been converted into a giant money box. (It's been painted with red and white stripes, like the lighthouse.) According to a notice on a little plaque screwed to the front, all the money collected from the old mine goes to The Grubtown Retired Lighthouse Keepers' Relief Fund, but I'm not so sure.

Gumshoe Slackjaw himself climbed out of the van, which he'd reversed so that the back doors were facing the beach. He opened these doors and lifted out two very large shiny galvanised buckets and began trudging down to the shoreline.

'Can I help?' asked Jilly Cheeter.

Slackjaw Gumshoe looked around. He didn't look thrilled to see her. 'Where's Mango Claptrap?' he asked. 'Aren't you two always together?'

'Not always,' said Jilly. 'I've got my dog, Harvey, with me this morning.

'And me,' added Hobo Browne.

The hardware store owner frowned, then handed one bucket to Jilly and the other to Hobo Browne. 'If you wouldn't mind filling them with seawater and bringing them back to the van, please,' he said, already on the way back there himself to collect some more empty buckets.

'What are you going to do with all this water?' asked Jilly Cheeter as she lugged her third bucketful up to the van.

'It's for filling one of the tanks at my aquarium,' said Mr Gumshoe.

'And carwash,' Hobo reminded him.

'And carwash,' Slackjaw Gumshoe agreed.

'But I thought the tanks were all full already?' said Jill. 'I was up there the day Farflung Heaps unloaded all the sea creatures into their new homes, remember?'

'I remember,' said Slackjaw Gumshoe. He avoided looking into Jilly Cheeter's eyes, looking instead at his feet.

Jilly looked down at his feet too. Although Mr Gumshoe was dressed in jeans and an old T-shirt (with the faded slogan **'GRUBTOWN IS BETTER THAN WERTY'** on it), he was wearing a pair of frogman's flippers.

Was Jilly imagining things, or did he suddenly look a bit shifty?

Like he had something to hide?

Chapter Five
The old switcheroo

The costumes were being delivered to **THE RUSTY DOLPHIN** at 9.00 a.m. precisely, so Mango Claptrap and Jilly Cheeter had arranged to meet there fifteen minutes before that.

Mango Claptrap was already waiting outside when Jilly arrived. He was dressed, as always, in his ridiculously short shorts and still had the turban-like bandage on his head.

'How are you feeling?' she asked him.

'Much better, thanks,' said Mango. 'The worst thing about having a clock land on my head is Vestige's corny jokes about it.'

'Such as?' asked Jilly Cheeter.

'Such as . . .' said Mango Claptrap thrusting a scrumpled piece of paper into her hand. 'I wrote a few down.'

Time doesn't just fly, it lands on your thick head, squirt.
WATCH OUT BELOW! Or should that be 'CLOCK OUT BELOW'(because you don't have a watch)?
I think that clock likes you. It's about to fall for you.

Jilly groaned. 'These are terrible,' she said.

'And they're the best ones,' said Mango Claptrap. 'You're very lucky not to have a big brother.'

Jilly Cheeter just has her dad – and Harvey the dog, of course – but they get along great. Jilly's mother, Dandy Cheeter, died when Jilly was just a few months old. There's a really nice photo in their hallway showing Jilly's mum holding Jilly as a baby. It's one of the first things you see when you go into their house.

The vintage **Gladrags & Stitch** van arrived at 9.00 a.m. on the dot. It was black all over, with beautiful gold writing. It was so clean and shiny that they must have been polishing it out of sight around the corner. There was no way that it could have stayed that gleaming clean, even after a short journey.

The driver was dressed in a black frock coat (which has long coat tails), and an off-white shirt with a starched collar. Jilly Cheeter and Mango Claptrap thought he looked dead posh.

Sitting next to him in the passenger seat was someone wearing exactly the same type of clothes but somehow managing to look an awkward and crumpled mess.

When Jilly and Mango realised who it was they were stunned. They couldn't have been more stunned if they'd grabbed hold of an

electric fence or eel.

IT WAS FASTBUCK FOX!

Never in a million years had either Jilly or
Mango expected to see one of the Fox boys
working anywhere other than at KILL ALL
DUCKS, let alone for the mega-famous
Gladrags & Stitch, but it was even more weird
for Jilly Cheeter because only a few hours
before she'd seen him falling over backwards
on the beach.

'Good morning,' said the driver, ever so

politely. 'My name is Blue-Ridge Handheld. Do I have the pleasure of addressing Miss Cheeter?'

Jilly nodded.

'Master Claptrap?'

'That's me,' Mango nodded.

'I have three packages for you,' said Blue-Ridge Handheld. 'Two containing bespoke costumes, and the third containing props.'

'Bespoke?' asked Jilly Cheeter.

'Made to measure,' said the man from **Gladrags & Stitch**. 'We were provided with your measurements.' He turned to Fastbuck. 'Mr Fox? If you'd be so kind?'

Fastbuck Fox went to the rear of the vehicle, opened the doors and climbed inside. It was a good few minutes before he reappeared with three large packages, labelled: *Miss Jilly Cheeter*, *Master Mango Claptrap* and *Gomez Heights Parade Props*.

When Handheld's back was turned, Fastbuck deliberately dropped the packages on Jilly

Cheeter's toe. This hurt quite a lot — she told me so — but she wasn't going to give him the satisfaction of knowing that so she swallowed her 'ouch'. He stuck out his tongue at her.

'We must away,' announced Blue-Ridge Handheld, climbing back into the driver's seat. 'Mr Fox?'

Fastbuck Fox climbed back into the seat next to him.

'Good day to you both,' said Handheld, and off they drove.

'Let's get these inside,' said Mango Claptrap. He took one end of the three packages and Jilly Cheeter took the other. They made their way into **THE RUSTY DOLPHIN** which was Gomez-Heights-Grand-Opening-Parade-Headquarters-For-The-Day.

The café's owner, Camshaft Thrift, was busy polishing mugs with a tea-towel behind the counter. Pageant Conquest was making last-minute checks on all the plates, dishes and bowls of food she'd prepared for the big day. Rambo Sanskrit seemed to have managed to get himself in a complete tangle with several big banners, and Officer Mustard Tripwire was doing his best to get him free (and getting *himself* in a right tangle in the process).

Jilly Cheeter and Mango Claptrap lifted the first package onto one of the empty tables. This was the one labelled *Miss Jilly Cheeter*. With Mango on tiptoe, looking over her shoulder, Jilly lifted off the lid and pulled back the tissue paper. Inside was what looked like a giant, flat egg.

'An egg costume?' she said in amazement. 'The mayor wants me to dress as an *egg*? What do eggs have to do with him moving into a knitted house? It makes no sense!'

'Let's have a look at mine,' said Mango. They put Jilly's package back on the floor and placed his on the table. He soon had the lid off, soon pulled the tissue aside and soon found that he

too was expected to dress as an egg.

'Weird,' he said. 'I just don't get it. Do you think we're supposed to be ducks' eggs?'

'Or pelicans' eggs?' suggested Jilly Cheeter. She knows how much Flabby Gomez loves Jip and Binkey and how upset he was when Binkey laid an egg which never hatched.

'But today is supposed to be a big celebration. Maybe the props will give us a clue,' said Mango Claptrap.

As it turned out, the props simply made them even more confused. It was a box full of life-size rubber chickens and joke eggs, some about the size of footballs. The rubber chickens made sort-of squawking noises if you squished them – certainly not clucking – and the eggs did a variety of different things. Some squeaked. Some had little plastic chicks poke out of the top. One even played a chickeny kind of tune.

Jilly looked at Mango.

Mango looked at Jilly.

'I just don't understand it,' she said.

'You don't have to understand it,' said Rambo Sanskrit appearing at their side with a clipboard. 'You just have to get dressed and ready. There's a cart for the props over by the hot chocolate machine.' He pointed with a bony finger.

Mango Claptrap and Jilly Cheeter carried the box of pretend eggs and chickens over to the shiny red cart and tipped them in.

Several miles from Grubtown there lies the town of Limp. It doesn't have a lighthouse and its town hall isn't nearly as big and impressive as ours. It does have a proper coastguard station with its very own helicopter, though. And, not only that, the townsfolk of Limp are very good at breeding chickens. And the very *best* chicken breeders in Limp are members of The Limp Chicken Breeders' Association. Here in Grubtown – and probably over in the village of Werty too – we laugh at the name

'The Limp Chicken Breeders' Association', because we think it makes out that the chickens they breed all walk with a limp. The people of Limp, however, don't find it in the least bit funny: firstly, because most things in Limp are called 'Limp this' or 'Limp that' and, secondly, a limping chicken is no laughing matter when you're a serious chicken breeder.

Anyway, it was in the nearby town of Limp that members of the Limp Chicken Breeders' Association – no giggling, please – were more than a little puzzled by the costumes they'd just had delivered for their Annual Cluck: two costumes made to look like giant balls of wool with a pair of giant knitting needles stuck through each of them.

There was also a huge sack of key rings. On one side of each key ring was a picture of a very flabby looking man with a big grin on his flabby face. On the other was what appeared to be – but surely not? – a knitted house.

'This isn't what I ordered,' said a very puzzled chairman.

'Maybe they couldn't read your handwriting on the order form,' said his wife. *She* never could.

What the Limp Chicken Breeders' Association

didn't know and what Jilly Cheeter and Mango Claptrap didn't know was that a certain Mr Fastbuck Fox had been switching labels on packages in the back of the gleaming **Gladrags & Stitch** van.

Chapter Six
Gomez Heights

There was a carnival atmosphere in the air when Flabby Gomez declared his new official residence, Gomez Heights, officially open. It came in big spray cans marked CARNIVAL ATMOSPHERE Special Economy Size, and Flabby's brother, Hacking-Cough Gomez, sprayed it everywhere just before the music started. It turned out that Hacking Cough Gomez has an allergy to CARNIVAL ATMOSPHERE in a can, so he had a terrible coughing fit.

At one stage he was coughing so badly that a few people thought that he might cough himself inside out, so they hurried off to get their cameras. The local papers★ pay good money for photos of stuff like that. In the end, Dr Fraud was called and he gave the mayor's brother a  cough sweet SO LARGE that there was no room in his mouth to cough. The small crowd which had gathered round burst into applause. Dr Fraud was then asked to move on by Constable Gelatine of the Grubtown Police, who knew that the mayor would be upset if anything but the opening of Gomez Heights was the centre of attention.

Flabby Gomez's speech was brief. He declared his new house open and then gave out free ice cream. He'd already declared a public holiday to mark 'this special day in Grubtown

★ *The Grubtown Daily Herald* and *The Grubtown Weekly Gerald*

History', but the free ice cream made him even *more* popular. Come election day, most of us probably would have voted for him but – as regular readers will already know – Grubtown is a town of one-man-one-vote, and the one man with that one vote is Flabby Gomez himself.

The mayor had wanted Grubtown's Fairly Good Brass Band to be playing throughout the event but they'd been frozen to an indoor ice-rink over in Limp (when rehearsing for the Limp Chicken Breeders' Association Annual Cluck) and unable to free themselves in time.

So Mayor Gomez had to make do with music supplied by Purple Outing, who was

happy to play a selection of old CDs and vinyl records from **PURPLE OUTING'S MUSIC SHACK**.

A particularly popular type of music in Grubtown is bwi-bwi, often spelt 'bwee-bwee.' It combines the rhythms of salsa and the beat of jazz-funk fusion with the charms of choral music and the buzz of a mosquito trapped in a rinsed-out jam jar. Or something. (I must confess that, although I'm big – 6ft 7in/over 2 metres tall – I'm *not* big on explaining different musical styles.)

Much of the music Purple Outing played was bwi–bwi and just about everyone was planning to party the day away.

Everyone in the parade was instructed to wear their costume throughout the day, even though it was to be mid-way during the event. before the free carnival rides were opened to one and all ...

... which is why Jilly and Mango mingled with the crowd dressed as a pair of unlikely eggs, wheeling around the big red cart of joke chickens and eggs. Their costumes looked even stranger because they'd been instructed to wear their medals as well. Large eggs with arms and legs pushing a big red cart are strange enough. Large eggs wearing medals were just plain *freaky*.

More than one baby burst into tears at the sight of them.

The costumes were bulky and both Jilly and Mango were soon suffering from the heat. 'No one's even going to be able to tell it's us in here,' Mango Claptrap complained. 'This is one of the mayor's stupidest ideas ever.'

Just then, Grabby Hanson strode over in his very best (full-dress) chief-of-police uniform. 'It's not safe wearing those medals in a crowd,' he said. 'They're very valuable and anyone could steal them. I suggest you take them off.'

They took his advice and, within a matter of minutes, the medals were promptly stolen from the place where Grabby had suggested the children put them for safekeeping. The thief was, of course, Grabby Hanson himself, our chief of police, so that was all right then. I don't mean it's all right for a chief of police to steal things. I simply mean that because it was Grabby who'd stolen them, Jilly Cheeter and Mango Claptrap could be sure of getting them back. Grabby always returns stolen goods to their rightful owners, which is why Grubtown's crime clear-up rate is so high.

Good old Grabby!

So everything was going fine at the grand opening until, that is, a great surge of water came out of nowhere, pouring down Clear-Day Hill.

It glugged.

It swirled.

It did generally wet, watery things.

It washed aside everything in its path (including Mrs Awning who was standing on a litter bin for a better view).

Before anyone knew what was happening, it had washed against the bottom floors of Gomez Heights.

If Gomez Heights had been an *ordinary* house, that would have been bad enough, with water-damaged furniture, carpets and a startled pet or two (with soggy fur or feathers). But we're talking about a KNITTED house here. And I can now report, with some authority, that knitted houses and water D-O-N-'T M-I-X.

Think of a giant sweater pulled out of a lake.

Think shapeless.

Think soggy.

Think *disaster*.

Chapter Seven
Big Man Gomez

Just about everyone used to be afraid of Flabby Gomez's dad, Big Man Gomez. Big Man Gomez was a nasty piece of work. He was a bully and had no manners whatsoever. He used to scratch himself in private places then sniff his fingers. He used make rude noises from both ends – sometimes at the same time – without so much as a 'sorry!' or 'I beg your pardon!' His official portrait shows him picking his nose. Sometimes, he'd also pick other

people's — noses, not portraits — without even asking.

Big Man Gomez used to own Grubtown before he gave it away in that raffle. When other people were talking at council meetings, he'd clean his ears out with a ball-point pen and then study the wax on the end. Before sucking it.

If anyone expressed an opinion that wasn't HIS opinion, he'd snort like a horse being offered a plastic carrot. He'd impersonate the way people spoke, exaggerating their accents and mannerisms, making everyone else out to be a lily-livered whiny so-and-so. Most people laughed (mainly in relief that he wasn't picking on *them*).

He also punched things: from furniture to flowers. Once he even punched a mountain. I'm delighted to report that, on this one occasion, his opponent got the better of him. Big Man Gomez was more hurt than the mountain. He wore a bandage around his sore knuckles for a couple of weeks. The mountain didn't even break into a sweat.

Big Man Gomez didn't bother to wash much. It's not that he didn't like baths or showers, he just liked the fact that no one dared tell him that he smelled, or dared suggest that he wash. It was like a silent (whiffy) challenge: *'I stink, but do you have the guts to say anything about it?'* Nobody was that stupid and when Formal Dripping (the official village idiot from nearby Werty) was in town, even *he* was sensible enough to know to steer clear of Big Man.

As I said, the man was really, *REALLY* unpleasant. When he died, just about everyone who'd ever met him was pleased. Flabby kept his father's ashes in a battered old coffee tin. When he'd lived in the mayor's official residence, Flabby had kept the tin on the mantelpiece in his living room. Whilst he was knitting Gomez Heights, Flabby and his family had lived in an eight-storey garden shed. During that time, the coffee tin had been on a shelf on the ground floor.

When they moved into the knitted house, Big Man Gomez's ashes were, of course, due to come too. But, somehow, they had gone missing.

Flabby Gomez's first thought had been that Grabby Hanson must have taken them, so he'd asked him. The chief of police had been outraged. He'd wished that he *had* thought of stealing them but, sadly, it'd been nothing to do with him.

The Gomezes had only occupied six floors of the shed. They'd used the seventh as storage, and the eighth was lived in by a bunch of lab rats. These were no ordinary rats. They'd been rescued from Doohickey & Squat Science Laboratories over in Werty. Their rescuer had been Emily Blotch, daughter of the then cleaner Condo Blotch (who is now the mega-rich mega-famous founder and owner of the **STOP BEING QUITE SO FAT** brand). These particular rats have impressively shaggy coats of fur and are very fond of classical music, except for anything by Brahms.

It seems to Flabby Gomez that these furry creatures understand him when he speaks to them, so he'd asked them if they knew about the missing coffee tin. The head rat, Free-Kick, had given a kind of ratty shrug, which had suggested to the mayor that they knew nothing about it.

'So I need you to find it, Chief,' Flabby Gomez had said to Grabby Hanson.

Grabby had nodded. 'I'll do my best, Flabby,' he had replied.

'In time for the grand opening of Gomez

Heights,' the mayor had said.

'I'll do my best,' Grabby Hanson had repeated.

But the grand opening, with its public holiday, short speeches, free ice cream and carnival rides and soggified house came, and there was still no sign of the tin containing the ashes of Big Man Gomez. And now Flabby Gomez was faced with the new problem of lots and lots AND lots of water.

When the water hit the house, people were puzzled that the water had come down the hill rather than from the direction of the sea. They assumed that it was a flash flood or the start of a storm.

My fellow Grubtowners thought that rain might follow at any moment, so stopped moving to the hypnotic rhythm of the bwi-bwi – also known as bwee-bwee, remember? – and dashed for cover.

Some sheltered in doorways, others under

the overhang of buildings, water lapping at their feet. A number of Grubtowners sheltered under copies of our local papers.* Some used parasols as umbrellas. Others used each other. (I spotted Derek Fox holding his son Mantle Fox over his head to keep dry.) Undertaker Wide Brim Petty-Mandrake stayed where he was. He would be protected from the rain – if it came – by the hat he always wears. It has a very wide brim.

Jilly Cheeter and Mango Claptrap stood under the large branch of an even larger tree. Dr Fraud produced a blanket from his impressive doctor's bag and held it above his head. Hacking-Cough Gomez removed the ENORMOUS cough sweet from his mouth and held *that* over his head. Mrs Awning, interestingly enough, stood under an awning.

Marley Gripe, the sign painter, decided to hold a fire bucket over his head. There were a number of sand-filled red metal buckets, with

* *The Grubtown Daily Herald* and
The Grubtown Weekly Gerald

the word **FIRE** stencilled on them in white letters, dotted about the place. Chief Grabby Hanson had ordered them put amongst the revellers because he was worried that a knitted house might catch fire rather easily. (He had been prepared for just about everything other than *water*.)

Marley Gripe simply tipped out the sand, planning to wear the up-turned bucket on his head. Only it wasn't just sand that fell out. So

did a large battered old coffee tin.

Grabby Hanson spotted this immediately and sprinted over to the spot in swift, handsome strides. He picked up the tin. 'You've found Big Man Gomez!' said Grabby triumphantly.

At the mention of that horrid man's name, Marley Gripe looked nervously over his shoulder as though he expected him to be standing there . . . even though Gripe knew that Big Man Gomez had been a long time dead.

By way of explaining, Grabby Hanson tapped the tin. 'His ashes, Marley,' he explained. 'In here.'

Marley Gripe heaved a sigh of relief.

'The mayor will be delighted,' said Grabby. 'Good job. Now scoop that sand back into the bucket, please, Mr Gripe, or I'll have to arrest you for littering.'

As I've said many times before, Grabby Hanson is an excellent policeman. He was glad Big Man Gomez's ashes had been found, but that wasn't the end of the matter. He still wanted to know *how* they'd ended up in the bucket in the first place. Who had put them there and, just as importantly, why?

'Do you know what?' asked Jilly Cheeter.

'What?' asked Mango Claptrap.

'This water is coming from the Grubtown Aquarium and Carwash.'

'How can you be so sure?' asked Mango.

'You have an octopus on your head.'

'Oh,' said Mango Claptrap.

What Jilly Cheeter had just said wasn't strictly accurate. In fact, not only did Mango have Dr Fraud's bandage on his head but also the domed part of the egg costume on top of that, so technically the octopus was on top of the eggy costume.

It wasn't the really big octopus they'd first spotted on the back of the lorry. This was one of the smaller ones she and Mango had watched Farflung Heaps lovingly place in the main tank (which had a tunnel in the middle

of it, so that visitors would feel as if they were somehow walking on the seabed, with the sea all around them).

Mango looked horrified. 'Then that means one of the tanks must have broken. The animals could be in danger. What should we do?'

'What can two children dressed as eggs do?' replied Jilly Cheeter.

'Get help!' said Mango.

'EXACTLY!' said Jilly.

Not surprisingly, the entire Grubtown Police Department was trying to calm down poor old Flabby Gomez who was terribly upset about his soggy house, though pleased to have his dad's ashes back. They ignored Jilly and Mango's yelps.

To be fair, there were quite a few other people yelping and splashing about. Some of them were having great fun. Others were looking for washed-away handbags, wigs and – in the case of Wide Brim Petty-Mandrake – a wide-brimmed black hat.

Jilly Cheeter and Mango therefore decided that they'd better DO SOMETHING now and ask for assistance later. If only they could find Mr Heaps!

One of the free carnival rides that everyone had been looking forward to, but had not yet had a chance to go on, was the spinning teacups. If you've never seen the spinning teacups, the name just about says it all. There are a number of giant teacups – big enough for two or three people to sit in each – which spin all over the place.

One of these cups had filled with seawater that must have poured over it.

Jilly Cheeter steered Mango Claptrap towards it. He was being extra careful not to lose his balance and let the octopus fall, like someone walking along with a book balanced on their head.

When they reached the cup, Jilly Cheeter

said, 'Bow your head.'

So that's exactly what Mango Claptrap did.

The octopus slid off the top of his egg costume and *splobbed* into the cup with a satisfying 'SPLASH!' (And *splobbed* is exactly the right word to describe it. I should know, I was there.)

'That should keep him happy for a while,' said Mango, 'but we should see if any other sea creatures need rescuing.'

'The props cart!' they both said at the same time. If they could fill that with water, it'd make an ideal rescue vehicle for any stranded sea creatures!

They dashed back to where they'd left it. It already had enough water in it for quite a few of the rubber chickens and plastic eggs to have bobbed out of the top. They were everywhere! Now Jilly and Mango tipped out the rest.

'We need more water!' said Mango Claptrap.

'No sooner said than done!' said Jilly triumphantly. She picked up one of the fire buckets, now full of seawater, and emptied it into the cart. Next, she tipped water from: Mrs Awning's best hat, a car hubcap, an empty popcorn tub and a litter bin.

'Good work, Jilly!' said Mango Claptrap. 'That should be plenty.'

They looked around at the terrible mess everywhere.

'I wonder what happened up there?' said Jilly Cheeter, looking up Clear-Day Hill towards the aquarium.

'Something bad,' said Mango Claptrap.

As our two intrepid egg-shaped heroes made their way up the hill, pushing the cart, they waded against an ankle-deep flow of water. They passed fellow citizens frantically rescuing all kinds of sea creatures, popping them into everything from a hurriedly emptied dustbin to a mug of seawater. Some slipped them into Jilly and Mango's mobile aquarium. They even saw a water-filled car, that must have been hit by the first big wave. It had a whole shoal of tiny fishes swimming around merrily inside. Partial Coggs was sitting in one of the front seats watching them, but he didn't seem too bothered. Perhaps he's good at holding his breath under water.

Jilly and Mango ran and ran and ran.

When they finally reached **THE GRUBTOWN AQUARIUM AND CARWASH**, they were panting for breath. Their water-filled cart was teeming with marine animals, by far the biggest being one of the great big eely things. It was *so* big that it was sticking out of the cart at both ends and, more than once, had fallen out on to the ground and had had to be picked up and put back in again.

'Someone!' shouted Jilly Cheeter. 'Anyone! We need to get this . . . this – er – great big eely thing into a proper tank!'

Mango gasped. He had just seen how bad the damage at the aquarium was. The whole main tank – the enormous one with the glass tunnel through it – was cracked in several places with water seeping through. It only had about a third of its water left. Near the top was a big hole where the first wave of water must have poured out.

There were some giant sticking plasters stuck in desperate 'X's across various parts of the glass, but it was clear from the terrible creaking and groaning that the tank walls were making that another hole might appear any minute!

Slackjaw Gumshoe was up a ladder frantically trying to stick brightly patterned wallpaper over some of the bigger cracks using a broom as a brush and treacle as paste. (It later turned out that he'd tried proper paste but it hadn't been nearly strong enough. The wallpaper had been in the back of his van, intended for his paint and hardware store.) The treacle had been provided by Pageant Conquest, who was now dashing over to Jilly Cheeter and Mango Claptrap. 'Bring that over to this side tank.'

Jilly and Mango hurried after her, wheeling

the cart behind them. It was surprisingly heavy with all that water and the creatures swimming around in it.

'I don't like the sound of that creaking glass,' said Jilly.

'I didn't much like the sound of the bwi–bwi,' said Mango with a grin.

'You know what I mean!' said Jilly.

Mango knew *exactly* what she meant. He was just trying to be brave and he knew that time was running out.

With the eel – if that's what it was – in a side tank, Jilly and Mango ran over to Slackjaw Gumshoe.

'What happened?' asked Jilly.

'How can we help?' asked Mango. He noticed a label stuck on the glass at knee height. It read:

REALLY TOUGH GLASS FOR AQUARIUMS
AND THINGS LIKE THAT.
YOU KNOW: REALLY STRONG.

'That's funny,' said Mango. 'More than one aquarium isn't "aquariums", it's "aquaria". You'd have thought people who make glass especially for aquaria would know that!' (The boy is full of useless information.)

The label was peeling away in one corner. Mango gave it a yank and it came off. Underneath, actually etched into the glass itself were the words:

REALLY THIN, CHEAP GLASS.

UNSUITABLE FOR JUST ABOUT ANYTHING

EXCEPT FOR WINDOWS IN PLACES WHERE THERE ISN'T MUCH WIND.

CERTAINLY NOT FOR AQUARIA.

Mango Claptrap would probably have been pleased that the people who'd genuinely made the glass – rather than the tricksters who'd stuck their own label over the top of it – had correctly used the plural 'aquaria' if it wasn't for the fact that it confirmed his greatest fear . . .

. . . that the tank might break under the weight of the water any time soon!

Chapter Nine
Pop and Stop

An extra pair of hands is always useful – and that's probably even true if you're an octopus – but, as luck would have it, Mango and Jilly ended up being far more than just that.

Soon there was a swarm of people dashing around the aquarium, frantically helping the poor sea creatures and trying to stop matters getting even worse. Pageant Conquest had been on the phone to her brother, Grabby Hanson, so soon he, Sergeant Gelatine and Mustard Tripwire had zoomed up Clear-Day Hill in the chief's police car and were running around looking very impressive in their uniforms. They even talked to each other through their cool police walkie-talkies, despite the fact that they were within easy shouting distance of each other.

At one stage, Officer Tripwire fired his potato gun in the air a few times. I'm not sure why but I think it was because he'd been wanting to fire it for ages. One of the potato-bullets bounced of a stingray's nose when it came back down to earth, but there was no harm done.

Farflung Heaps was there with the Angry Mob. They'd brought flaming torches and pitchforks, which are very handy if, for example, you're outside a castle trying to get a mad scientist to leave town who has built a living being out of old body parts. But flaming torches and pitchforks weren't much use now, so the mob tossed them into a pile, where the flames hissed out in the wet. This made the mob even MORE angry, so they shouted a bit, before angrily doing what they could to help.

Farflung Heaps was shouting instructions and, as head of the mob, everyone was used to doing as he said.

It really looked like the situation was under control, when a crack started to appear very near the bottom of the main tank. It may only have been a third full of water but it still contained thousands of gallons and, more serious than that, a huge number of creatures. If all the water escaped from here, the animals would be stranded – high and dry – and there wasn't enough room in the other tanks to save them all.

'Quick!' cried Slackjaw Gumshoe. 'Over here!'

Jilly Cheeter and Mango Claptrap were the first to reach him, just as the crack became a hole. 'Wedge me in there, feet first!' Mango shouted.

'*What?*' said Mr Gumshoe.

'Just do it!' said Mango.

Slackjaw Gumshoe and Jilly Cheeter grabbed Mango Claptrap – who was still dressed in his egg costume remember (with its tough outer shell and thick padding) – and jammed him into the hole.

It was like putting a cork in a bottle. He plugged the gap perfectly.

'Are you okay?' Jilly asked him.

'Fine,' said Mango.

'What about the jagged edges?' asked Gumshoe.

'I'm well padded in this egg,' said Mango, 'and they're what's holding me in place. Then he had a worrying thought. 'There aren't any sharks in this tank are there, Mr Gumshoe?' he asked, his feet in the water behind him.

Slackjaw Gumshoe shook his head. 'No, no sharks,' he said. 'We never put sharks in the same tank as the flesh-eating piranhas.'

Mango Claptrap gulped.

'A joke,' said Slackjaw Gumshoe, smiling for the first time in several hours. 'I think everything could turn out okay.'

And it did.

I am pleased to report that only one other serious hole appeared in the glass wall of one of the tanks. With so much water having already escaped, the pressure on the glass was far less.

Anyway, marine biologist Farflung Heaps and his team now knew that they had exactly the right thing to plug such a hole: Jilly Cheeter.

I've got the photographs from the local papers* in front of me now as I type, showing Mango and Jilly wedged in place (egg-round and grinning) in the glass wall of the aquarium, a few sea creatures peering through the glass in the water around them. Farflung Heaps and Slackjaw Gumshoe are proudly standing on the ground in front of them.

*The Grubtown Daily Herald and
The Grubtown Weekly Gerald

In the background of one photo, you can just make out Grabby Hanson stealing a walrus and hiding it in the back of his police car.

Gomez Heights dried out soon enough and all was well with the world. If you live in a wooden house, you worry about woodworm. If you live in a straw house, you worry about the Big Bad Wolf. If you live in a brick house, you worry about cavity-wall insulation. (If you've no idea what that is, then leave the worrying to someone who does.) So living in a knitted house isn't that different. It simply involves a different *kind* of worrying . . . such as RAIN and freak floods. But repairs are really, REALLY easy. All they require is a pair of knitting needles and the right amount of wool. It's the same if you want a few extra rooms or, say, a conservatory. You just get knitting.

Of course, the main problem with a knitted house is that it's very floppy. But, if you're as flabby as Flabby Gomez, flabby and floppy go together like – er – floppy and flabby. In that way, Gomez Heights reflects Flabby Gomez's personality. Who but such a flabby person would live in such a *floppy* house?

There are, of course, some rather naughty people in this particular GRuBtoWN taLe. One such person was Slackjaw Gumshoe. If he'd told someone about the teeny-weeny-and-very-slow leak in the main tank – which meant that he had to nip down to the beach some mornings and fill up some buckets with seawater to top up the water level – they might have pointed out to him that properly built aquariums – sorry, Mango: aquaria – shouldn't have even the tiniest of teeny-weeny-and-very-slow leaks. And that teeny-weeny-and-very-slow leaks have a nasty habit of becoming VERY big ones, just as this one proved. But he wasn't as naughty as some.

Fastbuck Fox would have been kicked out of his job at **Gladrags & Stitch** for deliberately swapping around those labels on the costume packages, but there was no need. He had made the switch to make Jilly Cheeter and Mango Claptrap look VERY SILLY INDEED. But what had happened instead? They'd saved the day *thanks to the costumes he'd made them wear.* This made Fastbuck Fox SO angry that he kicked the television when the story was reported on the local news. The television got stuck on his foot and the staff at the local hospital refused to help him get it off because they were sick of the Fox family and they all love ducks.

When Fastbuck turned up at the **Gladrags & Stitch** depot the following day, he was told by Blue-Ridge Handheld – very politely of course – that a television on the foot was 'unauthorised footwear' and, as such, not part of the acceptable dress code of someone working for the company. Fastbuck is now back behind the counter in a dead-end job at KILL ALL DUCKS, along with the rest of the family.

Another VERY naughty person was, of course, the one who pretended that the weedy glass was the strong stuff, suitable for building giant fish tanks. Hacking-Cough Gomez had bought the glass believing it to be the right stuff and had paid lots of (Gumshoe's) money for it. The police investigation is still under way, and Chief Grabby Hanson is confident of making an arrest soon. Mayor Gomez is really looking forward to giving the culprit a really big fine (which he will spend on wool for knitting a garage).

Which leaves a THIRD unpleasant person. You hadn't forgotten about Big Man Gomez's ashes mysteriously turning up in that fire bucket, had you? Chief Grabby Hanson hadn't. I'm pleased to report that the Grubtown Police Department finally got their man.

It was a woman.

It was Mrs Bunty Fox.

Grabby Hanson found her fingerprints all

over the tin and she soon confessed.

Here's what happened: when the removals people were taking the Gomez family's belongings out of the garden shed and into their removals vans, the coffee tin fell out of one of the packing cases. No one noticed. No one except Bunty Fox, that is, who was out walking her cat Scaffold. (That's the one she's trying to train to hate ducks as much as she does.)

Bunty quickly picked up the tin. She recognised it at once, so knew exactly who was inside it. She wondered whether she could hold it to ransom. Maybe she could force Mayor Gomez to ban all ducks from Grubtown or she'd tip his father's ashes into the sea? (See? I told you she's unpleasant.)

But then she caught sight of a trestle table at the side of the road. Next to it was a row of sand-filled red metal fire buckets. On the table was a tangle of bunting and a great big stack of leaflets about 'The Grand Opening of Gomez

Heights Today'. On top of the pile was a very large, smooth stone the size and shape of a loaf of bread, and *that* was what got Bunty Fox's attention.

She smiled. The huge stone looked SO like a loaf of bread that she was sure, if she painted it a bready colour, stupid ducks would think it was a REAL, 100%-genuine, loaf of bread.

Bunty was bursting with happiness and excitement. Just imagine it! She, husband Derek, and the children could all go to one of the local lakes, mingle with people feeding the ducks and throw the fake loaf to the water's edge. She could just imagine the ducks scrabbling out of the lake to reach it, then hurting their little ducky beaks on the stone. What a great day out that would be, laughing at ducks with injured beaks.

It'd be like Christmas and a birthday all rolled into one!

Barely able to contain her excitement, Bunty quickly hid the coffee tin in one of the many sand-filled fire buckets. She planned to come back for it later. Now she had her hands free to carry the loaf-stone home and get painting it a golden bready brown.

'I didn't *steal* Big Man Gomez's ashes,' she told Grabby Hanson once she'd confessed. 'You can't charge me with anything. I didn't commit a crime.'

'Wrong,' said the chief of police. 'I'm arresting you for littering. That stone was being used as a paperweight.' A grin broke out across his handsome face. 'When you took it off that pile of leaflets, six thousand of them blew away. . .'

But enough of these BAD folk, what about the poor sea creatures? Mr Jones and the three other drivers came back to **THE GRUBTOWN AQUARIUM AND CARWASH** and took them to various different temporary homes where they'll stay until the aquarium has been completely rebuilt. (They hope to re-open in about six months or so.)

As for the parade and free carnival rides, they did happen, just a few days later than originally planned. By this time, Grubtown's Fairly Good Brass Band had been freed from the ice-rink so were able to play for us. And who do you think sang a few songs for us, including a brand new one called '**There Was Water And Fish Everywhere Which Was Real Yucky, But We Were Saved By Some Giant Eggs, So We Were Real Lucky**'? Yup, the Grumbly girls. (Fortunately for me, I was able to stick the head of a rubber chicken in each ear.)

You might have expected Jilly and Mango to be dressed in their correct costume by then – two giant balls of wool crossed with knitting needles – but, no. They were the heroes of the hour and the mayor personally asked – well, *told* – them to wear the very costumes they had worn to block the holes. Jilly's father Sloop Cheeter beamed with pride and cheered from the sidelines with her dog Harvey, as did Mango's mum Carport Claptrap. His dad, Furl, as always, was busy doing one of his word-search puzzles. And brother Vestige? He was trying to out-stare a squirrel which had appeared on a branch to see what the fuss was all about.

Over in the town of Limp, the chairman of The Limp Chicken Breeders' Association was watching the whole thing live on television. (He'd sat down to watch the darts and had it on the wrong channel.)

He couldn't believe his eyes. There were two people wearing the egg costumes meant for him and his deputy at the Annual Cluck. The costumes looked battered and torn and appeared to be stuck together in places with strips of wallpaper and treacle . . . but they were

definitely what he'd ordered from **Gladrags &
Stitch**.

He called his wife into the room, pointing
at the red cart that Jilly Cheeter and Mango
Claptrap were pushing past the cheering
crowds.

'Look, Daphne!' he cried, in disbelief. 'Look
there. See? *See?*'

'See what, dear?' asked Daphne, putting on
her glasses.

'There!' he said, in utter disbelief. 'They've
even got our trick eggs and rubber chickens!'

THE END

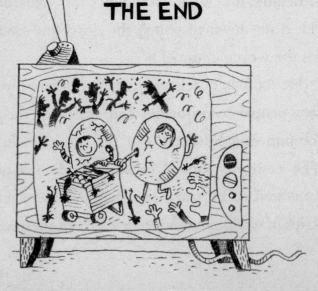

More words from Beardy Ardagh

Some people seem to think that I really am grumpy – even when I'm not – and some people seem to think that I'm just pretending to be grumpy – even when I'm not – in the hope that it puts you off writing to me about **GRuBtoWN taLes**. Grumpy or not, if you DO write, I suggest you address the envelope:

Beardy Ardagh,
c/o Faber & Faber,
Bloomsbury House
74–77 Great Russell Street
London
WC1B 3DA

and write **GRuBtoWN taLes** in the bottom left-hand corner.

If you're hoping for a reply, **DON'T FORGET TO INCLUDE A STAMPED SELF-ADDRESSED ENVELOPE**. (I'm not going to buy any stamps myself. I'd rather spend my money on important things such as bread and water, to STAY ALIVE.) Not that I can promise you'll get a reply, of course. I may peel off the stamps and use them to wallpaper a wall.

You can also check out my website at www.philipardagh.com, unless it's broken, which it probably will be.

(Just some of) the folk who pop up in GRuBtoWN taLes

Jilly Cheeter girl and one-time duck-gatherer

Mango Claptrap a short boy in short trousers, whatever the weather

Manual Org a smooth-skinned fellow

Flabby Gomez Mayor of Grubtown

Kumquat 'Grabby' Hanson the chief of police

The Grumbly girls the seven Grumbly daughters

Hacking-Cough Gomez the mayor's brother

Big Man Gomez the mayor's dead dad

Pritt Gomez the mayor's wife

Tundra Gomez the mayor's son and heir

Formal Dripping official village idiot for the nearby village of Werty

Derek, Bunty, Shaun, Mantle, Fastbuck & Garrideb Fox the duck-hating Fox family of humans (not foxes)

Rambo Sanskrit council job-giver-outer

Sonia Pipkin local builder

The troll inhabitant of Beardy Ardagh's airing cupboard

Mrs Awning town accident-waiting-to-happen, first name unknown

Minty Glibb owner of Minty's Cake Shop

Mickey 'Steamroller' Johnson doughnut-loving steamroller driver

Leggy Prune the future Mrs Johnson

Mrs Johnson the former Leggy Prune

Constable Gelatine a police sergeant

Mustard Tripwire an officer of the law and Gelatine's nephew

Galaxy Tripwire a train driver and former beauty queen

Relish Tripwire a tropical fish salesperson

Informative Boothe a very knowledgeable chap

Hobo Browne a gentleman of the road/smelly tramp

Camshaft Thrift owner of The Rusty Dolphin Cafe

Farflung Heaps self-appointed leader of an angry mob

Garlic Hamper the lighthouse keeper

Shoona Loose the world-famous singer who does a lot for animal charities

Tawdry Hipbone movie star

Snooks Miss Hipbone's pampered pooch

Luminous Shard bald heckler and mechanic

119

Carlo Monte the riverboat gambler

Lefty Scorn proprietor of Scorn's Laundrette
      & Jeweller's

Acrid Scorn an irresponsible dumper of hazardous
      waste

Jip the town pelican (official mascot)

Marley Gripe a painter of signs

Dr Fraud a pretend doctor (but he's cheap)

Sloop Cheeter Jilly's dad

Harvey the Cheeter family dog

Furl Claptrap Mango's dad

Carport Claptrap Mango's mum

Vestige Claptrap Mango's brother

Claws their cat

Partial Coggs Grubtown's resident artist

Slackjaw Gumshoe paint & hardware store owner

Purple Outing very rich owner of Purple Outing's Music Shack

Hind-Leg Outing amongst other things, mother of Purple's vast number of children

Wide Brim Petty-Mandrake a regular complainer

Hetty Glue-Pen cinema manager and projectionist

Condo Blotch former cleaner now head of her very own keep-fit and health-food empire

Emily Blotch Condo's daughter

Free-Kick leader of the escaped lab rats

Lulu Free-Kick's mate for life

Hardfast Tendril Grubtown's chief forester

Paltry Feedback a printer and cake decorator

Careworn Wormwood nine-day king of Grubtown

Glowering Silt general manager of Fettle's hotel

Avid Folklore manager of Fettle's hotel

Chevvy Offal owner of Offal's Sunbeds

Premix Stipend victim of one of Offal's sunbeds

Pageant Conquest food-maker (and Grabby Hanson's sister)

Mossy Edging a very fair judge who doesn't take bribes that often

Hybrid Byword the (now dead) TV chef

Limbo Goulash an office worker

Clam Wretching founder of Wretching's Dairy

Barton Wretching her son and current owner of the dairy

Beardy Ardagh honoured citizen of Grubtown and the teller of these tales

The delightful Beardy Ardagh tells of other GRuBtoWN taLes

There are important things in life and there are *un*important things. One of the most important things – if not THE most important thing – is ME. Something else which is important is that you read ALL of my GRuBtoWN taLes. Just to make absolutely sure that you've read each and every one of those published so far, I've taken the time and trouble to tell you a bit about them (except for this one), over the next few pages. Because I've taken the effort to write this, the least you can do is make the effort to read it.

RIGHT NOW.

Philip Ardagh

GRuBtoWN

taLes

Stinking Rich and Just Plain Stinky

GRuBtoWN taLes
Book One

StinkiNg Rich aNd Just PlaiN StiNky

or

A Diamond As Big As His Head

Grubtown is full of oddballs – from the singing Grumbly girls to a family of duck-haters, and an outsized mayor who's knitting a new house – but Manual Org is too repulsive even for them. Getting him to leave town is top priority, until the discovery of a humongous diamond changes everything.

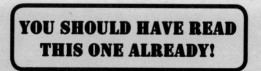

YOU SHOULD HAVE READ THIS ONE ALREADY!

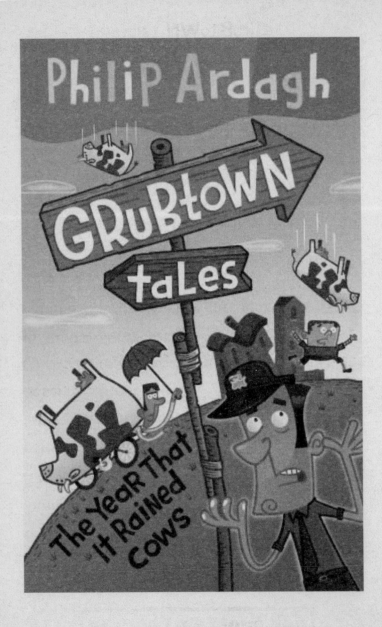

GRuBtoWN taLes
Book Two

The YeaR That It RaiNed Cows

or

That Well-Known Secret Door

A startled cow falling out of nowhere onto Limbo Goulash while he's riding Marley Gripe's bicycle marks the start of a chain of events strange even by Grubtown's standards. Soon damaged property includes **PURPLE OUTING'S MUSIC SHACK** and Minty Glibb's attempt at the world's largest (strawberry) jelly-trifle. With Mayor Flabby Gomez throwing a wobbly, all chief of police, Grabby Hanson, can do is have the cow-fearing townsfolk watch the skies. Underground, meanwhile, there lies another big surprise.

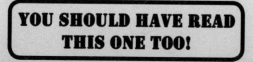

YOU SHOULD HAVE READ THIS ONE TOO!

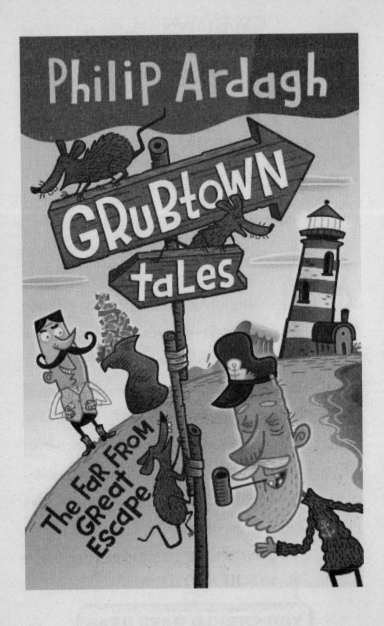

Philip Ardagh

GRuBtoWN taLes

taLes

The FaR FRoM GReat Escape

GRuBtoWN taLes
Book Three

The FaR FroM GReat EscaPe

or

The Light, the Switch and the Wardrobe

When the local lighthouse is plunged into darkness and a ship runs aground – flattening THE RUSTY DOLPHIN – it's hard to imagine things can get much worse in Grubtown. But then there's a jailbreak and the Police Department (all three of them) needs all the help it can get from the (often bonkers) townsfolk. No wonder more trouble is waiting just around the corner.

AND READ THIS ONE!

Philip Ardagh

GRuBToWN

taLes

The WRoNG
End of
the Dog

GRuBtoWN taLes
Book Four

The WRoNg
ENd of the Dog

or

The Pedal-Bin Pelican

When famous film star Tawdry Hipbone visits Grubtown for the world premiere of her latest movie, *For the Love of Ducks II*, Mayor Flabby Gomez couldn't be more excited but, as usual, nothing goes to plan. Miss Hipbone's dog, Snooks, is snatched by a low-flying pelican, and it's a race against time to find him, in a rescue attempt involving Grubtown's usual ragbag of bungling buffoons.

Grubtown Tourist Board

Visit www.visitgrubtown.com

Create your own Grubtown name, try your
hand at reporting for The Grubtown Daily
Herald and see what other silliness the tourist
board has in store for you.

Watch out for the ducks!